ISLE of YOU

David LaRochelle *illustrated by* Jaime Kim

CANDLEWICK PRESS

Was today a hard day?
Are you feeling sad?
Lonely?
Maybe even a little angry?

I'm sorry.
Come with me.
I know the perfect place to go.

It's there, just across the bay. Can you see it?

The Isle of You.

The boat is ready.

Step right up and dump all your worries into this basket. Shake them out of your pockets and brush them off your shoulders, every last one. You won't need to bring them along.

I'll wait till you're ready.

All set? Off we go!

Ahhh . . . That ocean breeze feels grand.

There's the welcoming committee, waiting with wide-open arms.

What would you like to do first?

Swim in the waterfall?

Ride a stallion across the sand?

Climb a mountain?

Hunt for treasure with some newfound friends?

There's even a giant eagle who would love to give you a bird's-eye view of the island.

Or maybe you'd rather stretch out on this
hammock for a while.
Take your time. The choice is yours.

The castle doors are open. Perhaps you'd like a change of clothes. Wizard robes, evening gowns, ninja masks, capes, crowns . . . the Hall of Costumes has it all.

Try something on.
Now take a look in the mirror.
Fabulous! You look fabulous!

It sounds like it's time for the evening's entertainment
to begin: dancing polar bears . . . on roller skates . . .
in tutus!

They've been practicing for weeks, just for you.

And look! One of them has made your favorite dessert.

Mmmmmm . . . It smells delicious.

Go ahead, help yourself.

The sun is starting to set.

Shall we take a walk on the beach?

If you're lucky, you might spot dolphins.

That's amazing—I've never seen so many starfish before!

Did you know that starfish like to grant wishes?

Pick out a starfish and give it a try.

There's the moon, whispering that it's time to head home.

Are you feeling better?

I hope so.

But before you leave, the polar bears have
something important you should know.
Lean closer and they'll tell you what it is:
Someone loves you very, very, very much.
It's true. Roller-skating polar bears never lie.

It's time to say your goodbyes. But don't worry—
you can come back whenever you'd like.

And the next time you're feeling sad, remember:

Isle of You.

For You

D. L.

For Dreamers

J. K.

First edition 2018

Library of Congress Catalog Card Number pending
ISBN 978-0-7636-9116-5

18 19 20 21 22 23 TLF 10 9 8 7 6 5 4 3 2 1

Printed in Dongguan, Guangdong, China

This book was typeset in Caecilia.
The illustrations were created using watercolor with digital tools.

Candlewick Press
99 Dover Street
Somerville, Massachusetts 02144

visit us at www.candlewick.com